"Nice catch," Bryan whispered to Lara. "But we were lucky to get out of that inning. Scouts for the baseball camp are here! We've got to find Sam!"

"And I just remembered something important," Lara declared.

"What?"

"Sam's grandparents are in Europe."

"No way!" Corey said.

"Yes, way," Lara said. "Sam told me the other day that his grandparents were heading to France for a couple of weeks. Even if one of them was in the hospital it would be in Paris or something—a little far away for him to make a quick visit."

"Wow!" Jack said. "This is serious!"

"It sure is," Bryan added, shaking his head. "Someone has done something to Sam."

Coming soon in the
Sports Mysteries series:

#2 The Haunted Soccer Field

Sports
M Y S T E R I E S

THE CASE OF THE MISSING PITCHER

T.J. EDWARDS

ILLUSTRATED BY CHARLES TANG

A
LITTLE APPLE
PAPERBACK

SCHOLASTIC INC.
New York   Toronto   London   Auckland   Sydney

ISBN 0-590-48452-4

Copyright © 1995 by Daniel Weiss Associates, Inc. All rights reserved. Published by Scholastic Inc. APPLE PAPERBACKS ® is a registered trademark of Scholastic Inc. Cover art copyright © 1995 by Daniel Weiss Associates, Inc. Illustrated by Charles Tang.

Produced by Daniel Weiss Associates, Inc.
33 West 17th Street, New York, NY 10011

12 11 10 9 8 7 6 5 4 3 2   5 6 7 8 9/9 0/0

Printed in the U.S.A.   40

First Scholastic printing, April 1995

To Dan Elish and Andy Packer

THE
CASE OF THE
MISSING PITCHER

THE JOKE'S ON SAM

"Come on! Come on! Hurry up!" Sam Jansen grabbed his baseball and glove as he raced for the classroom door. "Recess is only fifteen minutes. I've got to work on my curve before tomorrow's big game!"

Sam glanced over his shoulder and stopped. Corey was sitting cross-legged by her locker with her nose buried in a book. Bryan was leafing through a film magazine. Only dark-haired Jack, enthusiastic as always, was in motion.

Sam pushed the bill of his cap farther up on his forehead. "Corey," he said, "read *after* recess."

"One more paragraph and I'm there," she replied.

Jack rolled his eyes. "That paragraph better be short," he said. He turned to Bryan. "You too! Come on! Let's hit the field!"

Bryan didn't look up. Jack grabbed him by the arm and tried to yank him to his feet. But Bryan was a big kid—he couldn't budge him.

"Come on!" Jack cried. "Don't make me get tough with you, Bryan." He gave Bryan's arm one more heave. "Oh, forget it," he huffed. "Sam and I will just meet you out there."

"I'm almost done," Bryan said. "I'm just reading about this new movie where a circus clown falls in love with a trapeze artist." Then to himself he said, "Wow! How do they get the ideas for these movies?" Bryan had already shot three short films on his parents' camcorder. The best was *The Talking Rocking Chair,* a mystery about crime-solving pieces of living room furniture.

Bryan was also an amazing catcher. He played the backstop like Darren Daulton of the Phillies, and he could block the plate and chew ten sticks of gum at the same time.

He put down his magazine and pushed a few strands of red hair out of his eyes. Still in a daze, Bryan picked up his mitt and cap and wandered after Sam and Jack, toward the field.

"Finished!" Corey cried, and slammed her book shut. She picked up her official Barry Bonds baseball glove, her prize possession, and raced for the field. On the way out she caught sight of her reflection in the glass front door of the school. She liked to think she looked like Barry Bonds—same dark skin, same wide smile. Even more, she liked to think that she *played* like the San Francisco Giants' star.

"Future MVP," she said out loud, and hustled after Sam, Jack, and Bryan.

A moment later, Lara finally came sprinting out of the school, her blond hair flying behind her.

"What took you so long?" Sam called from the pitching mound. He whipped the ball to Corey at first base. "Hurry up!"

"I had to finish this detective book," Lara called, running up. "Sherlock Holmes—what a pro!"

"Man!" Sam exclaimed. "All any of you guys want to do is *read*. We have a huge game tomorrow morning. Let's get in a little extra practice!"

"Oh, please," Corey said with a smile. "We'll be ready."

Sam knew Corey was right. The five friends were great athletes, and they loved baseball. Together, they were the core of the Smithfield Community Center's baseball team, the Sonics. The team was made up of kids from different elementary schools in the district. Sam was the team's star pitcher. Bryan, of course, was the catcher. Lara played center field, Corey first base, and Jack second.

"The best team I've ever coached. The best team of ten-year-olds in Minnesota, for that matter!" Mr. Lester had declared. Their last victory had been a 12–3 slaughter that brought their season record to eight wins, no losses, and one tie.

Still, the five friends knew that tomorrow was the true test. At eleven A.M. they'd take on their arch rivals, the Johnsonville Hornets. Earlier in the season they had dueled to a 2–2 tie.

"Did you hear that the Hornets say the Sonics are a bunch of wimps?" Jack cried, fist clenched.

"Yeah!" Bryan said with a scowl. "I heard, all right!"

"Aw, they're nothing but a bunch of jerks," Corey said bluntly.

Bryan nodded. "That's one way to put it."

"Okay already! Can we please practice?

Please!" Sam said impatiently.

"All right," Bryan said, turning his batting helmet backward. "But at least let me get behind the plate."

"Now we're talking!" Sam yelled. "So who's gonna win tomorrow?"

"The Sonics!" Lara cried, grabbing a bat.

"All right!" Sam said. "Here comes my Nolan Ryan Express."

Lara was at the plate, digging her heels into the dirt. Her long blond hair blew behind her from under her batting helmet. Sam smiled.

"Wipe that grin off your face, Sam," Lara cried. "Don't even *think* you're going to blow one by me."

Bryan got into his crouch and held up his mitt. Sam reared back and threw. Lara saw the ball leave his hand perfectly and head straight toward the heart of the plate. Lara clenched her teeth, forced herself to relax, then swung and connected.

But where was the telltale crack of the

bat? The ball should have been soaring over the fence, but instead . . . it exploded!

"What the . . . ?" Lara exclaimed as hundreds of squiggly worms shot out of the ball.

The next five seconds were a blur. Lara heard Bryan howling with laughter, and then Sam, grinning like a madman, came trotting toward her.

"Disgusting!" Lara said. "Worms!"

"Not worms," Corey said as she ran over, laughing. "Spaghetti!"

"Really?" Lara asked.

"Yep," Corey said, pulling a piece off Lara's shirt.

"Spaghetti!" Lara repeated, picking it off herself. She looked at Sam. "I can't believe you did this. You actually put cooked spaghetti inside a baseball cover and sewed it up? It must've taken weeks!"

"Only a night, actually," Sam replied.

Lara shook herself and grinned. She could imagine how she looked—she was covered from head to toe with pasta.

"No hard feelings?" Sam asked, extending his hand.

Lara hesitated, then slapped Sam's palm.

"No hard feelings," she said. She wiped off her T-shirt. "All right, let's play ball! Come on!"

All during the final two periods of school, Lara thought hard about how to pay Sam back. That afternoon, in Mr. Ovid's gym class, the entire fifth grade was scheduled to play baseball. Lara had the perfect plan.

Mr. Ovid is cool, Lara thought as she tried to follow along in math class. *I'm sure he'd be willing to help. . . .* But she was going to need the help of everyone in the class, too. Between periods she spread the word.

Finally the bell rang, and it was time for gym. Mr. Ovid agreed to stay inside the school for five minutes while the class picked teams and warmed up.

9

That was his part of the joke.

Sam ran to the mound. "All right!" he called. "Get ready for some serious heat!"

He wound up and hummed in a high fastball to Jack at the plate. Jack got a piece of it, and the ball went flying past the shortstop. But instead of running for first, he ran for third!

"Hey!" Sam called. "What are you doing?"

"Mr. Ovid told us to do this," Jack called back.

"What?" Sam said. "Get out of here."

"No, it's true," Corey said, walking in from first base. "Mr. Ovid said it would help our skills if we did everything backward."

"But that makes no sense."

"That's what I thought," Corey said, "but he's the gym teacher."

"Why didn't he tell me?" Sam asked.

Corey shrugged. "Maybe he couldn't find you."

Sam shook his head but stepped back

up on the mound. He must have been the first pitcher in recorded history to get three outs with the batters running the wrong way!

"All right," Mr. Ovid said, walking up as Sam's team ran for the dugout. "Sam. Grab a bat. Get things started."

Sam put on a batter's helmet, took a few warm-up swings, and stepped into the batter's box. A certified meatball came right over the plate. Sam swung as hard as he could. The ball shot off the bat into right-center field. Sam took off . . . toward third, then second, first, and finally home. When he reached the plate, Mr. Ovid was standing there, hands on his hips.

"Sam!" he barked. "What in the world is the meaning of this? Your practical jokes are wearing thin, young man."

"*What*?" Sam said. "But you said . . ."

"I said what? I told you to bat, not make a—a mockery of my gym class!"

"But you told us to run backward. . . . Lara and Jack and . . ."

By now everyone was hysterical, even Mr. Ovid. Sam threw the batter's helmet onto the ground and stared at Lara. She was laughing so hard, tears were streaming down her face.

"Okay, okay," he said. "You got me. Happy?"

"Thrilled!" Lara gasped.

"Serious burn," Bryan said with a satisfied nod.

"Okay," Mr. Ovid said. "Let's take it again. And this time, Sam, why don't you try running toward first?"

WHERE'S SAM?

Mr. Lester pulled up at the Smithfield Community Center field Saturday morning at ten-forty, twenty minutes before the game.

"Coach!" Lara cried, running toward him.

Mr. Lester smiled and pulled a Smithfield Sonics' baseball cap over his bald head.

"Hiya, Lara," Mr. Lester said. "Read any good mysteries lately?"

Lara nodded. "Sure. Two a week."

"Wow," Mr. Lester said. "Two mysteries a week with fifty-two weeks in a year means you read one hundred and four mysteries each year. That's quite a bit. And if each mystery has two hundred and fifty words a page, and each book is about one hundred and fifty pages long . . . well, let's see." Mr. Lester pulled out his pocket calculator. He was an accountant and always kept one handy.

"Mr. Lester," Lara said impatiently, "we've got a problem."

"What . . . what was that? Oh, yes. A problem, you say? Well, I've got my calculator out, so tell me what it is."

"A problem that a calculator won't help solve," Lara explained.

Mr. Lester raised his eyebrows. "Really, now? No calculator . . . ? Hmmm . . . I wonder. Well, what is it?"

"Sam's missing." Lara said.

"What? But he's got a two-point-oh-four earned-run average!"

"I know! And the game starts in just

fifteen minutes. There's no way we'll win without him."

"Oh, I'm sure he'll be along."

"Hey, guys," Bryan yelled from the dugout. "Come here! Fast!"

Lara and Mr. Lester exchanged a glance, then hustled across the parking lot to the Sonics' dugout.

"What is it?"

"Look what I just found," Bryan said. "A note from Sam."

Mr. Lester held up a piece of pink construction paper and read the typed note aloud.

Dear Mr. Lester,

Sorry I can't be at the game. My grandmother in Minneapolis got sick, and we've got to rush to the hospital.

Good luck!
Sam

Mr. Lester scratched his head. "This is

most unusual. My statistics show that Sam has the highest attendance record of anyone on the team."

"I hope his grandma isn't too sick," Lara said.

"Well, she must be," Jack said, "or else Sam wouldn't go."

"Not with a game like this on the line," Corey said.

"Maybe his parents forced him," Bryan said.

"Wait a second here!" Corey said. "Does Sam even have a grandmother in Minneapolis?"

Lara snapped her fingers. "You know, he doesn't."

"Right," Corey said. "Sam has two grandparents living right here in Smithfield. I've seen them at some of our games. And his mom's father lives in Florida."

"Right," Lara said. "He and his family go down there for spring break."

"And he comes back totally tan, the bum," Bryan muttered.

"Well," Mr. Lester said, "let us not overlook the possibility that perhaps one of his grandparents here in Smithfield got sick and was taken to a hospital in Minneapolis. An accounting buddy recently informed me that Smithfield Medical Center sends thirty-nine percent of its cases to other cities . . . or was that twenty-nine percent?" He scratched his head. "Ah, well. I'll have to check the figures and get back to you."

"That's all right, Mr. Lester, don't sweat it," Bryan said.

Meanwhile, the rest of the team was gathering in the dugout. One of them was Peter, a lanky boy with an overly large Adam's apple. He was Sam's backup pitcher.

"What's going on?" Peter asked, loping over. "You guys look like your pet dog just died or something."

"It's almost that bad," Lara said. "Sam isn't here."

Peter suddenly looked nervous. "Really? Does that mean . . .?"

"That's right," Mr. Lester said. "You'll have to pitch."

Peter looked sick. "*Me . . . ?* But Sam has to show up, right? I mean, I saw him half an hour ago."

"You did?" Bryan asked.

"I got here early," Peter explained.

"When?" Mr. Lester asked. "Give me the exact time. Numbers, man! Numbers!"

"I dunno, around ten after ten. . . . I was just warming up—throwing pitches against the backstop—you know, in case I got in as a reliever or something. Anyway, Sam came motoring over, and I said, 'Hey, Sam,' and he said, 'Hey, Peter.' And I said, 'Ready for the big game?' And he said, 'Yup.'"

"He didn't say anything about *missing* the game?" Bryan asked.

"Not a thing," Peter said, shifting uneasily from foot to foot. "He headed toward the community center. That's the last I saw of him."

"Then maybe he did leave for Minneapolis," Corey said.

"What do you mean?" Peter asked.

"Sam wrote us a note saying he had to go to Minneapolis to see his grandmother," Jack replied. "He tacked it to the dugout."

"No kidding?" Peter said.

"I don't know," said Lara. "This sounds a lot like one of Sam's jokes."

"If Sam is playing another joke . . ." Jack said, shaking his fist.

"There's no need for violence, team," Mr. Lester said. "In the meantime, it would appear, Peter, that you will be our starting pitcher." He draped an arm around the boy's bony shoulder. "Just because your statistics aren't half as good as Sam's is no reason to be discouraged. Put the numbers behind you! So what if your ERA is six-point-one-seven? Who cares if opposing batters are hitting four-oh-three against you? What matters is what happens today. It is a well-known fact that . . ."

As Mr. Lester walked Peter to the mound, the four friends took off for the community center to change into their uniforms.

"I suppose we'll find out if it's a prank soon enough," Bryan said.

"Well, I think it's kind of weird," Jack said, opening the door. "I mean, Sam would never joke around about such a big game."

"Yuck!" Brian said. "What's that smell?"

"Paint," Jack said. "Mr. Leblanc's been painting the community center basement all week. I mean, who goes down there? Why bother?"

The friends walked down the corridor and into the gym. Just off the gym were the two changing rooms. Bryan stuck his head inside the boys' room.

"Sam's not in here," he said. "But wait—his clothes are!"

"His clothes?" Lara asked. "Hmmm . . . you mean his uniform, right?"

"No," Bryan said. "He must be wearing his uniform. His regular clothes are thrown in the locker he always uses. Why don't you just come in and see for yourselves? No one's in here."

The gang slowly walked into the boys' locker room.

"Well, this is strange," Lara said when she came to Sam's locker.

"What is?" Bryan asked, getting down on one knee.

"He *must* be hiding. No one would visit his grandmother in a hospital in his baseball uniform."

"Maybe *he* would," Jack said.

"Maybe," Lara said. "I guess if he was already in it and then found out he had to go . . . But why would he come to leave a note and then change into his uniform? It makes no sense."

"Something isn't right here," Brian agreed. "I'm with Jack—it doesn't seem

21

like Sam to joke about a game with the Hornets. Still, he must be hiding, or else . . ."

"Well, there's one way to find out," Corey said. "Call his grandmother and see."

Lara nodded. "Right. You wanna try, Corey?"

While Corey went off to find a phone, Lara, Jack, and Bryan changed and went back outside. Fans and family were filling the wooden bleachers. The Hornets were already on the field, warming up.

"Man," Bryan muttered to Lara, "what do those guys eat, raw steak for breakfast, lunch, and dinner?"

"They're huge all right," Lara said.

"I could take 'em!" Jack declared, flexing his biceps.

The Hornets looked like a team of eighth graders. They were pretty intimidating just whipping the ball around the field. Bryan, Lara, and Jack gathered with the rest of their team. Mr. Lester was finishing a pep talk and holding up a graph and a slide rule.

"And so," he said, "mathematics and statistical analysis clearly show us that despite the Hornets' superior strength and size, our team statistics better theirs in four out of six major categories. Have no fear! Now repeat after me: 'The numbers never lie!'"

The team shouted it out and Mr. Lester tacked the lineup card onto the dugout:

Jack Cummings: second base
Lara Martini: center field
Nelson Tory: third base
Corey Johnstone: first base
Bryan O'Malley: catcher
Marla Armstrong: left field
Peter Fisk: pitcher
Stanley Major: shortstop
Bobby Hershfield: right field
Reserves: Tom Blevis, Madeleine Rabb

Just then Corey came running from the community center. "I called Sam's grandparents," she said. "Nobody's home."

"Hmmm," Lara said. "That doesn't *prove* anything. Just because they aren't home doesn't mean his grandmother is in intensive care."

"One thing's for sure," Bryan said. "This is no prank. The game's about to start."

The four friends looked at one another in dismay. What was going on? Was Sam's grandmother really sick? Or was someone keeping him out of the game? Something didn't seem right. If only they could figure it out.

The umpire dusted off home plate. "Batter up!" he cried.

A Swarm of Hornets

"Come on!" Lara said. "We have to get this win with or without Sam."

The Sonics took the field. The home fans cheered, but Mr. Hanraddy, the old community center administrator, was the loudest. He was their biggest fan.

"Go get 'em, Sonics!" Mr. Hanraddy called. "I've got a dollar that says you guys take this one!"

"Betting the bank, huh?" Bryan yelled over.

"Well, I was going to go for five, but without Sam . . ."

Bryan stood behind the plate and adjusted his mask. Mr. Hanraddy was right. Without Sam, their chances were slim. He looked toward the mound. There stood Peter, all arms and legs, throwing the ball into his mitt.

He looks terrified, Bryan thought. *I'd better work the hitters myself.*

Bryan loved psyching out opposing hitters. As each batter stepped up, Bryan talked and talked, then talked some more. He made it difficult for even the most disciplined batter to concentrate.

But Bryan knew he would need to be in his best form today. Peter could throw hard, but didn't have much control and had no variety. No curves, no change-ups—not like Sam.

Jack chatted it up from second base. "He's no hitter! Easy out! Easy out!"

Bryan got into his crouch and watched the first player, a big kid with curly blond

26

hair, step into the batter's box. Bryan remembered from their last game that his
name was Morris.

"Nice haircut," Bryan said.

"What—what was that?" Morris asked.

"What? I didn't say a thing."

Bryan watched Peter go into an awk-
ward windup and release the ball. It was
headed directly over the plate and not all
that quickly. The curly-headed boy
whipped his bat around.

Crack!

Bryan threw his mask down and
watched the ball shoot over the center-
field fence and hit smack in the middle of
the parking lot on the other side. The
Hornets went wild. Bryan turned to pick
up his mask and saw Mr. Anderchuk, the
Hornets' coach, jumping up and down. He
was no bigger than most of his team.

"One pitch! One homer!" he called.
"What did I tell you, boys? Get our runs
one by one! That's all we gotta do. We'll
crush 'em!"

Bryan looked away, disgusted. Morris waved to the crowd as he rounded third. When he stepped on the plate, he glared at Bryan.

"Thanks," he said. "I like my haircut, too."

"Fret not, team!" Mr. Lester cried. "The statistical probability of a team opening a game with two home runs is slim!"

"Not with Peter pitching," Bryan said to himself. He brushed his foot across the plate. "Come on!" he yelled. Peter looked like a worn-out rag. "No big deal! Let's get this next guy!"

The next kid up was already in the batter's box.

"Come on, Kevin," Mr. Anderchuk yelled. "Just like Morris. Put it out of the park."

Bryan tried to size him up. Was he a patient hitter? Impatient? Did he have a good eye? He was certainly enormous. And dirty. His pants were streaked with black marks.

"Ever hear of laundry?" Bryan asked, pointing to his pants.

28

"I get dirty just warming up," Kevin snapped. "I'm tough!"

Peter wound up and threw. The ball thudded into Bryan's mitt about a foot outside the strike zone.

"Ball one!" the umpire cried.

The next pitch sailed over Bryan's head. Bryan picked up the ball and called time.

"Just aim for my mitt, Peter," he said, running to the mound. "We've got good fielders out there. Let 'em hit it. Our guys'll make the plays."

Peter swallowed. "Sure. In the mitt. You got it."

Bryan went back to the plate.

"Looks like this is going to be a great game," Kevin said. "Where's the guy who usually pitches for you? Chicken out?"

"Sam doesn't know the meaning of the word *chicken*," Bryan snapped, getting into his crouch.

"Then how come I saw him running off

before the game?" Kevin asked with a smile.

"You what?" Bryan asked, surprised.

"You heard me," the boy replied. "I was in the parking lot, and across the way I saw Sam tack some sort of a note to the dugout. Then I saw him take off like a scared puppy. Where I come from, that's a chicken."

"Can it," Bryan replied. "Sam loves to pitch, especially against bozos like you."

Peter released the ball, and it thudded into Bryan's mitt just outside the strike zone. Kevin swung wildly.

"That's a striiike!" the umpire called, gesturing dramatically with his right hand.

"What do you mean, 'bozos'?" the boy asked.

"Well, nobody but a bozo would swing at that pitch," Bryan answered. "You guys'll swing at anything."

The next pitch flew in, this time, miraculously, a strike. Kevin held off, though, just to prove to Bryan that he had a good eye.

"Hey, Kevin!" Mr. Anderchuk yelled. "Swing! You're a hitter up there—hit!"

Bam!

Peter's next pitch slammed into Kevin's shoulder.

"Ow!" he cried, and took a step toward the mound. "Moron!"

The umpire, a high school senior, stepped in front of him. "It was an accident, buddy. No fights, okay? Take your base."

Kevin shook out his arm and trotted toward first.

"Watch your inside pitches," the umpire called out.

Peter nodded. He looked like he was ready to pass out. The third batter walked to the plate. Everybody in the league knew Larry. He was a small kid, but a great player. He could hit, run, and field. Even Bryan had to admit he was the real stuff.

31

"Hey, Larry," Bryan said as the small boy dug into the batter's box. "How's tricks?"

"Tricks are great," Larry said, taking a practice swing.

The first pitch was way outside.

"Why is that?" Bryan asked, tossing the ball back to Peter.

"'Cause we're going to trounce you guys, that's why," Larry said with a smirk. "A real old-fashioned rout."

Larry took ball two.

"A rout, hmmm?" Bryan said. "Well, we've got some secret weapons."

"Oh, really?"

"Striiike one!" the umpire shouted.

"I'm not talking to you anymore," Larry said, and stepped out of the batter's box. But after taking a few practice swings, he stepped up to the plate and said, "Know what's best of all? Scouts from the baseball camp are here."

"Ball three!" the umpire cried.

Bryan barely caught the ball. He was shocked. This was news!

"You're kidding me!"

The camp was run in conjunction with the Minnesota Twins. The kids worked with the athletes from the Twins' minor-league system. But the only way to go was to be picked by a scout. Bryan looked toward Mr. Lester. Why hadn't he told them? Maybe he didn't know. Maybe he didn't tell them because he didn't want them to feel the added pressure. Bryan knew that the way Sam pitched, he would have had no problem getting the scouts' attention.

"Where are they?" Bryan asked.

Larry nodded toward the stands. A man and a woman wearing blue baseball caps were sitting in the bleachers, notebooks in hand.

Whack! Bryan turned back just in time to see Larry lace a double down the left-field line. By the time the Sonics got the ball back to the infield, Kevin was at third. Two runners were in scoring position and there were no outs! Bryan shook his head. Without Sam, the game was quickly becoming a disaster.

"Ahoy there," Bryan said weakly to the fourth batter, a hulking boy with a fake tattoo of a pirate ship on his right bicep.

The boy growled and knocked the dirt out of his cleats. He smacked the first pitch with a low, hard line drive that hit the dirt and bounced neatly into Corey's mitt. She stepped on first.

"Out!" the umpire cried.

But the play wasn't over yet. Kevin was sprinting home.

"Here!" Bryan called.

Corey whipped it to him and Kevin was trapped. He ran back toward third base, but Bryan threw to Nelson. When Kevin turned for home, Nelson whipped it back to Bryan. Bryan knew they had him. Kevin slid for third, but Bryan threw to Nelson in time for the tag.

"Out!" the umpire exclaimed.

The Sonics' fans cheered wildly. Double play! But Bryan knew they weren't out of trouble yet. Larry was still on second base, and the number-five hitter was at the plate. He looked like he meant business.

"You related to Paul Bunyan?" Bryan joked.

"Paul Bunyan? You mean the lumberjack?"

"Right," Bryan said. "You know, the one who was supposed to be thirty feet tall."

"I'm a distant relation," the boy said, cutting Bryan off. "But my side of the family is bigger."

Bryan knocked down the first pitch with his body. He didn't think he could rattle this kid, and he was too tired to shout anything to Peter.

The next pitch sailed in high, but the distant relation of Paul Bunyan swung. Bryan stood up and watched the ball sail deep into center field. Lara drifted back . . . back . . . back. . . .

Then Bryan saw her running toward the infield, her glove high in the air.

"Yes!" Bryan screamed. "Yes!"

"Not to worry, team," Mr. Lester said as the Sonics came in off the field. "I've done some calculations that may interest you. . . ."

"Nice catch," Bryan whispered to Lara. "But we were lucky to get out of that inning. Scouts for the baseball camp are here! We've got to find Sam!"

"And I just remembered something important," Lara declared.

"What?"

"Sam's grandparents are in Europe."

"No way!" Corey said.

"Yes, way," Lara said. "Sam told me the other day that his grandparents were heading to France for a couple of weeks. Even if one of them was in the hospital it would be in Paris or something—a little far away for him to make a quick visit."

"Wow!" Jack said. "This is serious!"

"It sure is," Bryan added, shaking his head. "Someone has done something to Sam."

4

A Clue in the Art Room

"It's time to open an official investigation," Lara said. "We'll start at the beginning—with the note."

She pulled it out of her uniform pocket and spread it out on the dugout bench. It was typed on a piece of bright-pink construction paper.

"That looks just like the paper we get in arts and crafts," Corey noted.

"Just what I was thinking," Lara said. "So whoever wrote this note had been in the art room, right?"

"Have we absolutely ruled out that Sam didn't type this note?" Corey asked.

"Why would Sam *type* us a note?" Bryan asked.

"Maybe he was in a rush?" Jack suggested.

"In a rush?" Bryan said. "If he was in a rush, he would've written it out."

"I don't know," Jack replied. "Maybe he couldn't find a pen."

"Or maybe," Corey said, "whoever wrote the note knew that we would recognize Sam's handwriting."

"That's it!" Lara said, jumping up. "Sam's handwriting is horrible. No one could imitate it. And if they didn't know Sam well, they wouldn't know what his handwriting *looked* like. A handwritten note would give it away in two seconds."

"But where does this leave us?" Bryan asked.

The kids exchanged a glance.

"Batter up!" the umpire yelled.

"Jack," Mr. Lester called over. "Grab a bat. Get us started!"

"Go ahead and bat," Lara said. "We'll keep thinking."

Jack grabbed a helmet and bat and jogged to the plate. The crowd cheered as he stepped in the batter's box.

"About time, shorty," the Hornets' catcher said. "Where were you? Playing handball against the curb?"

Jack smirked and took a practice swing. He dug in. The first pitch was fast but right over the plate, and Jack hammered it to right field. When the dust cleared, he was standing on third with a triple.

"You're batting four-fifteen now, Jack!" Mr. Lester yelled, punching numbers on his calculator.

"Man," the Hornets' catcher said as Lara stepped up to bat, "your coach is a numberholic!"

Lara laughed. "Well, I guess he is."

The Hornet pitcher stared her down,

and Lara got to work. The first ball came in low and away. Lara held off. The second was high and in. Again, she didn't bite. The third ball—that was her pitch. Lara kept her eye on it and connected.

Crack! She watched the ball loft high into center field. A burst of cheers came from the stands. The Hornets' outfielder drifted back and made the catch, but Jack had plenty of time to tag up and score.

Jack and Lara exchanged high fives with each other and the team.

"Attagirl, Lara!" Mr. Hanraddy called. "Way to bring him home!"

"One to one!" Mr. Lester cried. "All even!"

The four friends conferred as Nelson strode to the plate.

"We've got to get to that art room," Lara said. "We can't afford to wait until the game is over. Maybe Sam is there, or there'll be a clue about who wrote this note."

"Well, I'm up after Nelson," Corey said.

"Then it's Bryan's turn. We can try and slow the game down. You know, we can take lots of practice swings between pitches, that sort of thing, while you and Jack go check out the community center."

Lara looked worried. "But what if you guys strike out and we have to take the field?"

"I'll say you had to go to the bathroom," Corey answered. "Now move it!"

Lara and Jack sprinted across the field toward the community center. The minute they were through the door, Mr. Leblanc, the janitor, came bustling toward them. *"Allo!"* he cried in a thick French accent.

"Hello," Jack said.

"Mon Dieu!" he cried, fingering his thin mustache. "Your shoes! Zey are covered with ze mud!"

Lara pulled Jack onto the mat in front of the door, and they wiped their feet.

"Sorry 'bout that, Mr. Leblanc," Lara apologized. "We were in a rush."

The janitor smiled broadly. "Zis is no problem! But what are you doing here now? I t'ought you are playing ze baseball."

"We are," Jack said. "In fact, we're kind of in the middle of things."

"You see," Lara said, "we're in a difficult spot, you might say."

"What is it you mean? How can I help?" the janitor asked, wrinkling his brow.

"We're looking for Sam," Jack said. "You know him, right? Black hair. Good pitcher. Great curveball."

"Sam!" Mr. Leblanc said. "But of course! He is a fine young man. He pet my dog once. He compliment my sweeping. Help me to put away ze ladder. *Magnifique!*"

"Have you seen him?" Lara asked.

"Have I seen him? But of course! He was here earlier," Mr. Leblanc said, looking down and scratching his head. "Ah, now I remember! I had just opened ze building. I was cleaning ze gym, and I see Sam run out. He told me zat he was warming up for ze game."

Jack and Lara looked at each other.

"Is somezing ze matter?" Mr. Leblanc asked.

"Well, yes," Lara said. "Sam isn't here now. No one has seen him except you and Peter."

"Is Peter pitching, zen? He's wanted zat for some time. He is my nephew, you know. A fine boy!"

"Yeah, he is," Lara answered. "And yes, he is pitching. And he'll be really mad if we aren't back to take the field. Can we go upstairs? We have to check out something in the art room."

"*Absolument!*"

Jack and Lara followed Mr. Leblanc upstairs to the art room. They waited impatiently while he searched through the keys on his key chain for the right one.

"Come on!" Jack whispered.

"*Voilà!*" Mr. Leblanc said. "Here it is."

He held up a gold-colored key and opened the door.

Once they were inside, it didn't take long for them to find what they were looking for. On one of the desks was a piece of pink construction paper with a square cut out of it.

"That's the type of paper the note was on, all right," Lara said.

She took a quick glance around the room. "Any typewriters in here, Mr. Leblanc?"

"Typewriters?" the janitor answered. "No—a computer in ze back. You would like to see it?"

"Sure," Lara said.

Mr. Leblanc led them to the computer at the back of the room.

"There's no printer," Jack noted.

"Zis is correct," Mr. Leblanc said. "I have her taken to ze workshop two days ago. It printed ze letters crooked."

"Are there any typewriters in the center?" Jack asked.

"But of course," Mr. Leblanc said. "In some of ze offices on ze first floor."

Lara looked around the room some more. "Did you clean this room last night?" she asked.

"Of course! I am Monsieur Leblanc—ze King of ze Clean!"

Lara laughed.

"Did you empty the trash?" Jack asked.

"*Mais oui!*" he said, nodding.

"What is it?" Lara asked Jack.

Jack reached into the trash can and pulled out a bubble-gum wrapper that read: *Hubba Dubba Grape.*

"That must have been thrown out after you cleaned the room, Mr. Leblanc," Lara said. "Do you know who has been in here?"

The janitor shrugged. "Ze center is empty as far as I know."

Lara was about to ask more questions when Jack glanced out the window.

"Oh, no," he said, pulling at Lara. "The game! We'd better hustle."

Lara wanted to ask more questions. But Jack was right. If they weren't back to play the field, they'd forfeit the game. The case of the missing pitcher would have to wait.

"Thanks, Mr. Leblanc," Lara said, rushing out the door. "You've been a great help."

"But of course," the janitor called. "*Au revoir!* Be careful! Watch ze mud on my clean floors!"

5

Suspects

"Striiike three!"

"Okay, Sonics, let's get back out in the field," Mr. Lester shouted.

Lara and Jack had arrived just in time.

"What did you find out?" Bryan asked, running in from second base, where he had been stranded.

Lara quickly filled Corey and Bryan in on what she and Jack had discovered. Bryan stalled as he strapped on his pads.

"So whoever nabbed Sam *did* get the pink paper from the art room," Bryan said.

"Right," Lara agreed. "And they were probably chewing grape gum. They also had to find a typewriter, and Mr. Leblanc says the only ones in the center are in the first-floor offices."

"But I still don't see who would want to do anything to Sam," Jack said.

"Well, anyone on the Hornets," Lara said.

"Especially the better players," Bryan said. "Sam's our best player. With him out of the way, the Hornets are sure to have a better chance of being noticed by the scouts."

"Anybody else?" Corey asked.

Lara looked across the field. "Maybe Peter? He's always wanted to pitch."

"Yeah," Jack said. "And he said he saw Sam earlier."

"Mr. Anderchuk, maybe," Bryan said, turning his batting helmet backward. "He's more into the game than his team is. He would do anything to win."

"Right," Lara said. "We've got to keep our ears and eyes open."

49

"Come on, Sonics, let's hustle!" the umpire cried.

"See if you can find out anything more from Peter," Lara whispered to Bryan as she took the field. "Maybe he's not telling us something."

After Peter took a few warm-up throws, Bryan ran the ball back to the mound.

"What's up?" Peter asked, toeing the dirt nervously.

"Just throw strikes," Bryan said.

"I know, I know," Peter said. "It's just that I've never pitched a whole game before. It's tough. Boy, I wish Sam were here."

"You do?" Bryan asked, surprised.

"Sure I do," Peter said. "Why shouldn't I? He's our best pitcher, right? And this is a big game, right? We want to win, don't we?"

"Yeah . . . but I always thought you wanted to pitch."

"Well, sure. But not in such a big game. Those guys are bigger than Godzilla."

"Will you kids hurry it up?" the umpire yelled.

"Come on, Sonics!" Mr. Hanraddy cried, standing up in the bleachers. "Let's put a goose egg on the old scoreboard, you hear?"

Bryan hustled back to home just as the third baseman dug into the batter's box. He was chubby, but he looked powerful. The Hornets were all clapping and cheering.

"Come on, George, little hit now!"

"Love your new pitcher," George said. "Better not hit me, though, or I'll be forced to charge the mound, spin him around on the tip of my bat, and toss him into the next county."

"Sounds like you're scared," Bryan said.

"Me?" George said. He turned to Bryan just as strike one whipped across the plate.

"Why, you!" George said. "You did that on purpose!"

"Did what?" Bryan asked innocently. "I was concerned. You seemed worried that the ball would hit you. It's a perfectly natural fear."

"I'm not scared of anything!" George declared.

Peter wound up again, and Bryan held his mitt on the inside part of the plate. For once, Peter's aim was true. The ball ripped across the inside corner, and George jumped back out of the way.

"Strike two!" the umpire called.

"That almost hit me!" George cried.

"George," Bryan said, "you gotta relax."

The next ball was way outside. George lunged for it and swung.

"Striiike three!"

George wheeled around and slammed his bat in the dirt.

"I think your turn is over," Bryan said, whipping the ball to Nelson at third.

"You messed with my mind," George declared. "Hey, ump. He messed with my mind. Isn't there a rule about that?"

"Nope," Mr. Lester said, hustling over, leafing through the one-hundred-page Little League rule book. "Psychological intimidation is not mentioned."

"He's right," the ump said, pointing to Mr. Lester.

"Well, how about this?" George cried, picking up his bat.

"Are you crazy?" the umpire said, grabbing the bat. "You can't swing a bat at someone! You are out of here, mister!"

And then Bryan noticed something— George's teeth were purple! Bryan thought of the Hubba Dubba gum wrapper. Had George been in the art room?

"What do you mean?" George cried. "You can't throw me out!"

"Watch me," the umpire said. "You're out of here!"

"What's the meaning of this?" Mr. Anderchuk cried, storming over.

"I'm enforcing the rules."

"That's right," Mr. Lester declared, pointing to the rulebook. "Section seven, paragraph four, line thirty-three reads: 'Umpires may throw players out for their unsportsmanlike conduct at their own discretion.'"

"Right," the umpire said. "So you see, Mr. Anderchuk, I can toss your batter, and I can also toss you."

"I'm taking this up with the commissioner," Mr. Anderchuk shouted. His face was turning red. "It's not fair!"

The umpire smiled.

"You think this is funny, smart aleck?" the Hornet coach ranted.

"Well, can I stay in the game?" George asked. "He messed with my mind."

"Did you, Bryan?" Mr. Lester asked.

"Well . . ." Bryan said. "I suppose so. . . . It was just a little ribbing. Okay, okay. I'm sorry. I was just joking around."

"It should be against the rules," Mr. Anderchuk stated.

"Well, it isn't," the umpire replied. "You can say anything you want. This is the United States. We have freedom of speech.

But we don't have the right to hit each other with baseball bats."

Bryan nodded at the ump. He wasn't scared of anyone. Mr. Anderchuk looked defeated.

"If you apologize," the umpire continued to George, "I'll let you stay in the game."

George glared at Bryan, then forced a smile.

"Sorry, man."

"Sure," Bryan said.

Mr. Anderchuk took George by the arm, and the two stalked toward the Hornet dugout.

"Hey, George," Bryan said. "Where'd you get the gum?"

George wheeled around. "Listen, man," he said. "I said I was sorry. Get your own gum."

Bryan sighed. No luck there. "All right," he called. "Let's get these guys."

But a moment later the next Hornet was standing on second with a double.

Luckily, the next one hit a liner right at Jack. Two outs! But the ninth hitter beat out a grounder to third. The Hornets had runners on first and second with their leadoff man, Morris, stepping up to the plate.

"Here comes trouble," Bryan muttered, remembering his game-opening homer.

Morris backed off the first two pitches, both outside.

"He scared of me?" Morris asked.

"Nah," Bryan said.

Morris was all over the next pitch. The ball was going deep, deep into center field. Lara ran back, but she hit the fence way before the ball hit the ground on the other side.

It was 4–1, Hornets. Things were getting desperate. Lara saw Peter slam his mitt to the pitcher's mound. She was determined to concentrate even harder on the case. They needed Sam, badly.

There was the pink note, the mystery

typewriter, the gum wrapper . . . Then something clicked. If Mr. Leblanc had the keys, how did the kids who wrote the note get into the art room? Maybe Mr. Leblanc had let them in—and if he did, then he had to know who they were!

She had to get off the field and tell her friends. Getting a third out had never seemed more important.

"Come on, Peter!" she yelled. "Get this guy! You can do it! Two out! Two out!"

She saw Kevin, the boy who had been hit by a pitch, stride to the plate. Even from center field, she could tell that Peter's first pitch was way outside.

"Let's go!" Lara yelled again.

But three balls later, Kevin was standing on first. He grinned and blew a purple bubble.

"Hey," Corey asked. "Where'd you get that gum?"

"Don't try to distract me," he barked. "I know your team's dirty tactics."

Lara sighed. The inning looked like it

might go on forever. And now Larry was up, their best hitter.

With a full count, Larry lined a hard shot into the hole between first and second. Lara ran to back up Jack as Jack lunged for it. The ball just nicked Jack's glove and rolled deep into right field. Lara cut off the throw at second. She was practically jumping out of her skin.

"Get a stinking out!" she cried.

Finally it happened. The Hornet with the fake pirate-ship tattoo overswung at a sweet pitch. Lara saw the ball dribble to Peter, who easily threw the batter out at first.

"It's about time!" Lara cried, and ran to the dugout.

COREY INVESTIGATES

"I had an idea out there," Lara said as the team gathered. "How did whoever wrote the note get into the art room in the first place?"

"That's right," Jack said. "Mr. Leblanc had to open it up for us."

"Looks like someone has to question Mr. Leblanc again," Bryan said. "But I discovered something, too. George had purple teeth. I bet he's been chewing Hubba Dubba Grape."

"And I saw their second batter, Kevin,

blowing a purple bubble!" Jack exclaimed.

"Great," Lara said. "So we've got two prime suspects."

"I'll go talk to Mr. Leblanc," Corey volunteered.

"Striiike three!" the umpire called.

"There goes Marla," Lara said. "You'd better hurry, Corey. We'll try to delay things."

Corey took off across the field. She was the fastest runner in the fifth grade and was inside the building in seconds. She found the janitor mopping the playroom.

"Mr. Leblanc!" she called.

"*Mon Dieu!* You scare me!" he exclaimed. "How is ze game?"

"We're hanging in," Corey said. "But listen. Something is mixing us up. You had to let Lara and Jack into the art room with your keys, right? Did you lend your keys to anyone else this morning?"

"*Oui.* As a matter of fact, I was getting ze changing room ready when my nephew asked if he could go to ze equipment room for ze practice balls. So I give him ze keys and he bring zem back."

"Peter, huh?" Corey said. "Thanks a lot. You've been a big help."

"But Peter was not the only boy I give ze keys," Mr. Leblanc said.

"What?"

"George was with him."

"George!"

"Yes, George. Such a nice boy. He is one of Peter's best friends. A fine *artistc,* you know."

"He was with Peter when you gave out the keys, huh?"

"*Absolument!*"

"Thanks."

Corey started back toward the field but figured she had a little more time. Hadn't Mr. Leblanc told Lara that the only typewriters in the community center were on the first floor? Maybe she could peek in the windows and see if anything looked strange.

She took off at a sprint, rounding the building, peering in the windows.

But Mr. Leblanc had done his job too well. Each office was spotless. Not so much as a pencil was out of place. Corey shook her head.

Man, she thought, *this is no help at all.*

She rounded the far side of the building, expecting to find nothing. But then she saw something funny: a window was open.

She looked inside. It was a simple office with a wood desk, a cabinet, and a typewriter. As her eyes got used to the dark, Corey was able to see more and more. She pushed the window all the way up and leaned inside.

"Wow!" she whispered. There were small cakes of dirt with perfect holes in them on the floor. There was no doubt about it: that mud came from the bottom of cleats.

On the desk was a beat-up manual typewriter. Then her heart jumped. The typewriter ribbon was a tangled mess. She noticed there was ink all over the outside of the typewriter. It looked like whoever had used it last had had major troubles. They had probably gotten ink all over themselves.

Corey made a mental note of what she'd found, and dashed back to the game.

She was out of breath when she arrived. "What's happening?" she huffed.

"Bobby has a one-and-one count, and Stanley hit a single," Lara said. "What did you find out?"

"Good news." Very quickly she told the gang that Mr. Leblanc had lent his keys to Peter and George.

"Peter?" Bryan said. "Really?"

"That makes Peter a prime suspect now," Lara said.

"Yeah," Bryan agreed, "but that also makes him a great actor. When I talked to him on the pitcher's mound, he told me he wished Sam were here. He acted like he didn't want to pitch at all."

"Aw, he's always wanted to pitch," Jack said. "I bet he's faking, to throw us off the trail."

"It's possible," Corey said. "But I found out something else, too."

As Corey was telling Lara, Bryan, and Jack about her discovery of the open office window, Bobby banged a sharp grounder up the middle. The second baseman fielded the ball off a tough bounce, forced Stanley out, then threw to first. Double play!

"Well," Lara said, "looks like we can't do anything more now. We'll just have to keep our eyes open for more clues."

"And play tough baseball," Bryan added. "Pretty soon we may be so far behind, not even Roger Clemens would be able to get us back in the game."

UNANSWERED QUESTIONS

"Let's go, Sonics!" Mr. Hanraddy yelled.

It was the top of the third. The Hornets were leading 4–1.

"Let's get this guy," Bryan called.

But the first pitch Peter threw sailed over Bryan's head and slammed into the backstop.

"Most definitely a ball," the umpire said.

Bryan was losing hope fast. "Come on!" he shouted. "You wanted to pitch, at least try!" He tossed the ball back to Peter.

Peter looked confused. "I am trying, Bryan," he shouted, and reared back to wing one in for a strike.

"There you go," Bryan said. "Hum 'em in here!"

The Paul Bunyan look-alike took a mighty swing at a fat pitch. He just missed the sweet spot and popped out to Corey at first.

"Attaboy, Peter." Mr. Hanraddy was on his feet.

"All right, Peter!" Bryan yelled. "One down, two to go."

Then Bryan smiled. The next batter was George, the one who had nearly gotten booted from the game; the one with the purple teeth; the one who had borrowed the keys. Bryan was determined to get some information out of him.

"I don't want any of your talk," George said as he came to the plate. "I mean it!"

"Okay," Bryan said. "Not a word."

Bryan began to hum "Take Me Out to the Ball Game."

"I thought you weren't going to say anything," George said, turning around.

"I'm not saying a thing," Bryan insisted. "I'm just making beautiful music."

"Striiike one!"

"You're mixing me up again," George cried.

Bryan kept humming.

"Stop that!" George demanded as he took a vicious swing.

"Striiike two!" the umpire cried.

"Stop what?" Bryan asked.

"Your humming!" the ump said.

"Huh?" Bryan said, looking behind him.

"Why don't you just let him hit in peace?" the ump went on. "Is that how you want to win, by bothering every batter who comes up?"

Bryan swallowed hard. "Well..."

"Besides, you're off-key," the ump said with a smirk.

George gave a satisfied nod and faced the pitcher. Bryan sighed. What a day.

"Striiike three!"

"That stinks!" George threw his helmet against the dugout.

"Hey," Bryan called as George stalked back to his team. "Where'd you get that gum, anyway?"

George turned around, steaming. "What is it with you and gum? I forget where I got it, okay?"

"Okay," Bryan said. "But what were you doing in the art room?"

George's eyes bulged. "What? The art room . . . ?"

"Yeah. What were you doing there?"

"What is this? Twenty Questions?" He slumped on the dugout bench.

He's as guilty as they come, Bryan thought.

"Two dead," the umpire said. "Next batter!"

The next Hornet, Jim, pounced on the first pitch and laced a double to right center.

The Hornet pitcher stepped up to the

plate and, after working a two-and-two count, lofted a pop fly to shallow center. Lara dashed forward, mitt outstretched. Out of the corner of her eye she saw Jack and Stanley hustling back from the infield.

"Call it!" Mr. Lester shouted.

"Mine!" Lara called.

"I got it!" Stanley cried.

"No, mine!" Jack yelled.

Lara dove forward, bumped into Stanley, and they both fell to the ground. The ball plunked down right between them for a single. Jack fielded the ball and whipped it home, holding Jim at third. There were runners at the corners.

"Cheap hit," Lara said, brushing herself off.

The leadoff hitter, Morris, was up next. Peter pitched around him for a walk. Kevin, the guy he had hit in the shoulder, walked as well, forcing a run home.

"Five to one, Hornets!" the umpire announced.

Bryan called time and marched to the mound.

"Listen, Peter," he said, "you've got to throw some strikes."

"They'll hit them if I do!"

"If you don't, you'll put them on base anyway."

"Okay, okay—I'll try."

"Good," Bryan said, and headed toward the plate. Halfway there, he wheeled around. "What do you know about Sam, anyway?" he asked.

"Huh?" Peter asked.

"Do you know where he is?"

"How in the world would I know?" Peter asked.

"Oh, come off it," Bryan said. "You know where he is. You said you saw him this morning. Why would he just disappear?"

"What are you trying to do?" Peter asked, suddenly very angry. "Get me to confess? This isn't some stupid detective show. This is real life. Yeah, I saw Sam, just like I said, and that's it!"

"Then what were you doing with George getting keys from Mr. Leblanc?"

"Getting balls to practice with!" Peter cried. "You know—*baseballs?* Man! Shut up and get back down there. I'm ready to pitch."

Bryan stomped back to the plate. But Peter was right about being ready to pitch. He struck out the next batter, Larry, on three straight throws. The inning was over. Bryan watched Peter walk over to the dugout and sit angrily at the end of the bench.

"Excellent job, Peter!" Mr. Lester said. "That brings your strikeouts-to-batters-faced ratio to one out of every thirty."

Bryan sat beside Corey and the others. "I think I may have blown it with Peter." He told his three friends about the conversation.

"Weird," Jack said. "Maybe we should just search the whole building. Sam's probably in there somewhere."

"That'd take too long," Corey said.

"Well, let's get some runs back anyway," Lara said.

"Nickel-and-dime 'em!" Mr. Hanraddy called. "Make it happen!"

"Good old Mr. Hanraddy," Bryan said. "Our most loyal fan. Gets here a full hour before every game."

"He is a nice old guy," Lara said.

Jack dug into the batter's box, then laid a perfect bunt down the first-base line.

"Safe at first!" the umpire cried.

"Nice one!" Mr. Hanraddy exclaimed, jumping up and down. "Let's score us some runs! I got a dollar riding on you, and don't you forget it."

8

RUNNING BASES

Lara saw Jack taking a lead off first as she stepped up to the plate. She was determined to get on base. They needed to catch up, but even more, she hoped to learn something from the Hornets. The first pitch was low, and Lara held off. She rubbed dirt on her hands, gripped her bat tightly, and fouled off the next two pitches. One ball and two strikes.

"Come on, Lara!" Mr. Lester called. "A hit puts your season average at three-ninety-three!"

The next pitch was low, but she swung and lined it over the shortstop's head. Lara ran hard and slid into second under Larry's tag.

"Safe!" yelled the umpire.

Jack was holding at third.

"Hey," Lara said to Larry, brushing dirt off her jersey.

"Hey," Larry replied. "Nice hit." He smiled. "For a girl . . ."

"Well," Lara said, suddenly noticing a white splotch on his shirtsleeve, "at least I don't let birds take target practice on me."

Larry looked at his arm. There was a white splotch that could very well have come from a bird.

"What can I say?" he said with a grin. "Everyone likes me. Even birds."

"Striiike three!" the umpire called.

Lara realized she hadn't been paying attention. Nelson had struck out, bringing Corey up to the plate.

"Come on, Corey!" Jack shouted from third. "Bring me home!"

Lara took a slight lead. She glanced back at Larry, who was in a crouch, ready to field anything hit his way. Then she noticed something: his pants were covered with dark dirt stains. Not just a little, but a lot.

That's strange, Lara thought.

Crack! Corey lined a single to center. Jack flew home, and Lara rounded third.

"Home!" Mr. Lester cried.

But Lara thought better of it and stopped at third. Besides, George was the third baseman, and she wanted to have a little chat with him.

"Could've scored," George said.

"Maybe," Lara said. She hesitated. "So, George, tell me, where'd you get your gum?"

George looked flustered. "What is it with you guys and gum? You guys are crazy! I got it from Kevin. There. Happy?"

Lara nodded. "One more thing," she said. "What were you doing in the art room?"

George looked very uncomfortable.
"The art room?"

"Yes," Lara said. "Look, it's really weird that Sam has disappeared. We just want to find him."

Lara looked over her shoulder. Bryan was walking back to the dugout for a different bat.

Good, Lara thought. *He's stalling.*

Lara looked back at George. Then she got tough. "Face it, you went into the art room with Peter and helped him write that phony note from Sam. Then you stashed Sam somewhere so you could win the game. Right?"

George looked genuinely upset. "I didn't do any of that!"

"But Mr. Leblanc told us he gave you and Peter the keys. What did you do?"

"I can't tell," George said, his face turning beet red.

"You'd better," Lara said. "I have proof you were in the art room—a Hubba Dubba gum wrapper."

Bryan was at the plate now. He held off a pitch for ball one, then strolled away from the batter's box and pretended to knock dirt out of his cleats.

"Come on," the umpire said. "Let's hurry this along."

"Look," George said, "I just wanted to see the artwork you guys were doing for the state competition next week, okay?"

"What?" Lara asked. "I don't understand."

"I'm entering the art contest," George said. "My teacher at our community center says I'm really good—that I have a real shot at a prize. I just wanted to see what the competition was, that's all."

"I didn't know you were an artist."

"Now you do. Maybe I shouldn't have gone into your art room, but I didn't kidnap Sam."

"But how can I be sure you're telling the truth?" Lara asked.

"Well," George said, "I guess you can't."

"Was anyone else with you?"

Whack! Bryan connected, and the ball went flying into center.

"Was anyone else with you?" Lara asked, heading down the baseline.

"Larry was there, too," George called. "Peter let us in and left right away. Larry took off a minute later."

"Run!" Mr. Lester cried.

Lara tore home and slid over the plate a second before the ball thudded into the catcher's mitt. The Sonics were within two. She brushed herself off and told Jack what she had found out. Corey was on second, and Bryan stood on first.

"An artist!" Jack said. "Wow. I didn't know artists were so big."

"Artists come in any size," Lara commented.

"But is George telling the truth?" Jack asked.

"Well, Mr. Leblanc did tell Corey that George was interested in art, but I guess we can't be sure his story is true. I think I believe him, though."

"Who did it, then?" Jack asked.

"I don't know," Lara said. "It sounds like Peter. He's got a good motive. He's wanted to pitch all year."

"I think you're right," Jack said. "But there's one thing: If Mr. Leblanc lent Peter the keys to all the offices in the center, why in the world would he climb through a window to get to a typewriter?"

Lara nodded. "You're right. That doesn't add up."

"Maybe Larry did it," Jack said. "With no Sam, he's probably the best player here." He looked toward the scouts scribbling notes in the stands. "He wants to go to that summer camp pretty bad."

"And don't forget that George said Kevin was the gum supplier," Lara said. "Maybe he was in on it, too."

"And George may be lying," Jack said. "A lot of evidence still points his way."

Lara scanned the field. Larry was playing second, George was at third. Across the way, Kevin was playing first. Why couldn't she put it all together? Sherlock Holmes would have had it figured out by now.

Marla had just walked, so the bases were loaded. Lara looked toward home plate. Peter was in the batter's box.

"Striiike!" the umpire called, gesturing wildly with his right arm.

"A hit will bring Corey home!" Mr. Lester called.

Peter dug in. The Hornet pitcher wound up. Just then Lara stood up. There was a white splotch on Peter's uniform, too.

"What is it?" Jack asked.

"Ball one," said the ump.

Lara walked to home plate. "Hey, Peter."

"What?" Peter said.

"What's that stain on your leg? A bird get you?"

"This?" he said, pointing. "It's paint. I bumped into the wall of the supply room at the community center."

"Really?" Lara said. "There's wet paint there?"

"Yep."

"How long ago did Mr. Leblanc—"

"Listen," the ump cut in. "I'm sure this is all very interesting, but we're in the middle of a game here, okay?"

Lara backed away. The Hornet pitcher wound up and heaved a perfect pitch right down the heart of the plate. Peter took his bat off his shoulder and swung hard.

Crack!

The ball lined off his bat.

"All right!" Lara shouted.

The first baseman lunged to his left, but the ball was already in right field. Corey was home in a flash, and Bryan was rounding third, showing no signs of slowing down. The Hornet right fielder rifled the ball to Larry at second base, but Marla beat the throw.

"Home!" Mr. Anderchuk cried.

Larry threw a perfect strike. Bryan slid headfirst, and the catcher nailed him with the tag.

"Yer out!"

But the play wasn't over yet. Marla had made it to third, but the Hornet catcher saw Peter hustling to second. Quick as a flash, the catcher threw to Larry, who tagged Peter out, too.

"That wraps it up!" the ump cried.

Peter kicked the dirt.

"It's all right," Mr. Lester cried. "Let's hold 'em now."

As the Sonics took the field, the scoreboard read: HORNETS 5, SONICS 4. Lara saw the two scouts nod their heads toward Larry. He was an impressive ballplayer—a fine hitter with a deadly arm.

"Nice going, Larry," Mr. Anderchuk said as his star jogged back to the dugout. "You're halfway to that summer camp."

But Lara and the gang didn't have time to worry about the scouts. They had a game to win. *If we can just stay in this thing until we find Sam, we'll be okay,* Lara thought. *If I can only put the clues together in time . . .*

9

CLUELESS

Unfortunately for the four friends, they didn't get anywhere during the top half of the fourth inning.

Lara was doing brain gymnastics in center field, going over every Nancy Drew and Sherlock Holmes mystery she had ever read.

What would old Sherlock do in this instance? she thought. *Hmmm . . . it's not so elementary. The paint stains suggest that Peter and Larry were in the basement together. But George and*

*Kevin are the ones with purple teeth.
And what about that typewriter and the
open window?*

Behind the plate, Bryan tried to go
through every mystery movie he had ever
seen. But Bryan was having trouble
thinking about the game and the case at
the same time.

"Catching takes it out of you," he muttered to himself. "It's hard to think with
all this gear on."

At first base, Corey tried to think
through the problem logically. She was
still stumped.

We're definitely missing something,
she thought. *But what?*

At second, Jack, too, was lost in
thought.

Amazingly, a nifty unassisted double
play by Stanley at shortstop held the
Hornets scoreless.

But they didn't get any more runs or
clues in the bottom of the fourth. In the
fifth inning, the Hornets hammered out

two more runs. The Sonics, once again, went down without even getting a runner into scoring position. Going into the final inning of the game, the scoreboard read: HORNETS 7, SONICS 4.

"This is a disaster," Bryan said, putting on his mask. "Behind by three, and still no Sam."

Lara nodded. She looked defeated. She stared at the Hornets gathering in their dugout. "What a drag."

She slumped on the bench and put her head in her hands. When she looked up again, she noticed Peter walking to the other end of the dugout, rubbing his right arm.

"Tired?" Mr. Lester asked, draping an arm around his shoulder.

Peter nodded. "Yeah. I'm a little stiff."

"You want relief?" Mr. Lester asked. "I could ask Lara or Nelson to sub for you."

"Well," Peter said, "I'd like to try and finish. Could we wait and see how I do?"

Mr. Lester nodded, then turned to the

team. "Take the field!" he cried. "Just remember, team, that we are undefeated in games where the opposing team scores less than eight runs. Let's hold 'em!"

Peter jogged to the mound, rubbing his right shoulder.

"Hold 'em!" Corey shouted. "We can make up four runs with our last licks."

That number soon rose to six. Peter was fading fast. He gave up two more runs on only seven pitches! The Hornets were slamming everything that came their way.

Kevin whacked a liner down the first-base line. The Hornets' fans cheered wildly.

"That's it, boy," Mr. Anderchuk called. "Go for two!"

Lara ran in to back up Jack. The ball came in, and Kevin hit the dirt.

"Safe!" the umpire called.

"Darn!" Jack cried. "So close."

Lara sighed. What a nightmare. Smiling, Kevin stood up and began to

wipe off his pants. Lara was just about to head back to center field when she noticed something funny. Beneath the dirt on Kevin's pants were darker stains. Something clicked. Hadn't Bryan said that Kevin's pants looked dirty before the Hornets had even taken the field? She remembered the stains on Larry's pants. She thought about the messed-up typewriter ribbon Corey had seen in the first-floor office.

Things were beginning to add up.

Mr. Lester called time and approached the mound.

"How are you feeling, son?" he asked Peter.

The pitcher shrugged. "Pretty tired."

"Well," the coach replied, "I suppose I should pull you. But don't worry, you've done a fine job. According to my calculations, your ERA will decrease by nineteen percent."

As Mr. Lester motioned for her to come pitch, Lara suddenly knew what she must do. Drastic measures needed to be taken. Lara realized now that she couldn't wait until the end of the inning. Sure, she or Nelson could pitch, but they needed Sam now—anyone else would literally throw the game away. They were behind 9–4—this was serious.

Lara felt her heart thumping a mile a minute. What would Sherlock Holmes do in this situation? Lara knew that when he had a case cracked, he presented his evidence and let the police bring the crooks to jail.

Well, she thought, *if that's how Sherlock operates, I guess I can, too.* With a deep breath, she hustled toward the infield.

"Ump!" she cried. "I need a minute to say something."

"What?" the umpire said.

"I need time out," Lara said. "Time!"

10

LARA CRACKS IT OPEN

"What is this?" Mr. Anderchuk cried. "Delay of game! Get back onto the field and take your medicine."

The umpire shot Mr. Anderchuk a look, then turned to Lara. "What's going on? Are you hurt?"

"Nope," Lara said. "But I've got something important to say."

"Not now!" Mr. Anderchuk said. "Aw, this is what happens when you let girls play."

"First of all," Lara fumed, "girls can

play sports. And second, I suppose you don't care that two of your players are cheaters? Or maybe you know something about it?"

"What is this nonsense?" Mr. Anderchuk said.

"Lara," Mr. Lester cut in, "this is highly irregular."

"Maybe so, Mr. Lester," Lara said. "But this is an irregular situation!"

"Wow," Bryan whispered to Jack. "She's really on a roll."

"She sure is," Jack said. "But don't forget that she's read a whole heap of detective novels. She knows what she's doing."

"I hope so," Bryan said. People from the stands were beginning to gather around them.

"All right, all right," Lara said. "It seems I'm going too fast for some of you. Mr. Lester," she asked, turning to her coach, "may I please see the rule book?"

"Of course," Mr. Lester said.

"I suppose that there is a section in

this book that allows a game to be called on account of foul play?" Lara said, looking for the contents.

"Section seven, page fifty-six, paragraph nineteen, line twenty," Mr. Lester said immediately.

"Man, you sure know that book!" Mr. Hanraddy said, with a laugh, from the sidelines.

"Here we go," Lara said, stopping at the appropriate page. "It says: 'Game may be called if unsportsmanlike conduct has been proved.'"

"Okay," the umpire said. "You've made your point. What's so unsportsmanlike?"

"Larry and Kevin kidnapped our starting pitcher!"

Lara's accusation came as a total shock. Most everyone had assumed that Sam was sick or out of town. Mr. Anderchuk threw a helmet and pulled at his mustache. Mr. Lester began fiddling with his calculator. The rest of the Hornet and Sonic players pushed onto the field.

"Are you sure you know what you're doing?" Bryan asked Lara.

"I hope so," she whispered.

"This is nuts," Larry said. "I have no idea where Sam is."

"Me neither," Kevin said, stepping forward. "I told Bryan earlier that before the game I saw Sam tack a typed note to the dugout."

A wide smile spread over Lara's face.

"She's got an idea," Corey cried. "I'd know that face a million miles away."

Lara's eyes were sparkling. She took a step toward Kevin. "How did you know that the note was typed?"

Kevin's face fell. "Huh?"

"You heard me," Lara said. "How did you know it was typed?"

"Right," Bryan cut in. "You told me you were standing in the parking lot when Sam put up the note. You'd need binoculars to see it clearly."

"W-well . . ." Kevin stammered. "I just assumed it, that's all."

"Assumed it?" the umpire said. "Why in the world would a fifth grader type a note?"

"That's what I was thinking," Bryan said. "Especially if that particular fifth grader was in a big hurry, like you said Sam said he was."

There was a moment of silence. Kevin fidgeted back and forth.

"So what are you saying?" the boy asked. "That I typed a *made-up* note?"

"Not just you," Lara said. "Like I said: Larry was in on it, too."

"No way!"

Lara smiled. "If you weren't messing around with typewriters," Lara said, "then why are your pants covered with ink?"

"I—I don't know," Larry said.

"I found an open office window on the first floor of the community center," Corey said, stepping forward. "There was mud from cleats on the floor, and the typewriter ribbon was messed up."

"That was my typewriter!" Mr. Hanraddy exclaimed, stepping forward. "A minute before game time, I went to my office to drop off some papers and found that somebody had mucked up my ribbon pretty good. It was torn up so badly, I was planning to go back and fix it after the game."

A collective "ahh" rose from the crowd. Larry and Kevin stared at the dirt.

"Oh, really?" the ump said. He glanced at Larry and Kevin. "Go on. . . ."

Bryan stepped forward. "It makes sense," he said. "Look at these fresh black streaks on Kevin's pants legs. I noticed them the first time he got up. I mean, why would someone have fresh black marks on their pants before we even started to play? Anyway, remember how inky the note was—like it had been written on a messed-up typewriter? Well, I say Kevin and Larry got the ink on their hands when they typed the note and then smeared the evidence all over their pants!"

"I didn't type any note," Larry insisted.

"Then there's the matter of the wet paint," Lara said.

"Wet paint?" Mr. Anderchuk said. "What in the world does that have to do with anything?"

"Both Peter and Larry have paint splotches on their uniforms," Lara said. "That's what. The only place they could have gotten them is in our community center basement. I'll bet Sam is locked away somewhere down there."

"So Peter was in on it, too?" the umpire asked.

"No way!" Peter cried, throwing the ball into the dirt. "I had nothing to do with it."

"Well," Lara said, "I think we may owe Peter an apology. But he did *look* like a suspect. After all, he let George and Larry into the art room with Mr. Leblanc's keys. But it doesn't add up. If Peter were guilty, he would have used the keys to get into Mr. Hanraddy's office—he wouldn't have had to climb in through a window."

"I'm innocent!" Peter declared again. "Okay, so I let George into the art room to check out some paintings—I admit it. But then I went straight to the supply room, returned the keys to my uncle, and came out to warm up. That's when I saw Sam heading into the community center."

"He's telling the truth," Mr. Hanraddy said, waving his cane. "You all know I'm a big Sonics' fan. I arrive a good forty-five minutes to an hour before each game."

"Really?" the umpire said.

"That's right, sonny," Mr. Hanraddy replied with a nod. "I saw Peter warming up just like he said. And while Peter was warming up, I saw Sam walk into the community center to get changed."

"There," Peter said. "Just like I said. Mr. Hanraddy is my witness. I didn't leave the field once for forty minutes before game time."

Bryan patted Peter on the shoulder. "Sorry, man."

"So here's what happened," Lara explained. "Peter borrowed the keys from Mr. Leblanc, his uncle, then let George and Larry into the art room. After Peter left, Larry cut out a piece of pink paper. While George was still looking at our pictures, Larry and Kevin did something to Sam around the freshly painted part of the basement. Then they broke into Mr. Hanraddy's office and typed the fake note on the pink paper."

"Well," the umpire said to Lara, "now that we all know what's going on, I'm glad you stopped the game." He turned to Larry and Kevin. "What do you say we suspend you boys indefinitely? No more games this season, and that includes going to the all-star summer camp!"

"But—" Kevin cried.

He looked to the stands, where the scouts stood frowning.

"No buts!" the ump said. "That's final."

"Now let's get Sam back," Mr. Lester said.

Larry took a sheepish step forward. "You might want to try the closet in the supply room. . . ."

11

FREE AT LAST

Moments later, Lara, Bryan, Jack, Corey, and the umpire were watching Mr. Leblanc fiddle with his keys in front of the community center supply room.

"Lucky you remembered that Mr. Leblanc had just painted down here," Corey said.

"Yeah," Lara replied.

"*Mon Dieu*," Mr. Leblanc said with a shudder as he played with the lock. "Locking up a nice boy like Sam—and to win a game. Zis is insanity!"

With those words, he pushed the door open. There was a terrific banging at the far end of the room.

"The broom closet," Mr. Leblanc said.

"Not the greatest place to spend a morning," the umpire said.

A chair had been jammed against the doorknob.

"Let me outa here!" cried a familiar voice.

Corey and Jack exchanged a high five.

"Maybe we will," Bryan said. "And maybe we won't. What'll you give us?"

"A fat lip if you don't get this closet open," Sam yelled.

Lara moved the chair away and opened the door. Sam was smiling.

"Hey, guys. What took you so long?"

"Larry and Kevin locked you in, right?" Lara asked.

Sam nodded. "Yeah. I changed into my uniform and headed down for a baseball. That's when they shoved me in here. I thought it was just a joke at first."

"Right out of a movie," Bryan said. "Do you feel up to pitching?"

"Are you kidding?" Sam said. "Of course I do. What's the score?"

"Nine to four," the umpire said, "Hornets. Top of the sixth."

"Whoa," said Sam. "Not good news. Well, I'll try and hold 'em and hope we can get the runs back."

"Of course," the ump said, "I could ask the league for a forfeit, and give the Sonics the victory."

"Win by a forfeit?" Sam asked. "No way. We can get back six lousy runs."

"You tell 'em!" Corey said.

"Hey, Sam?" Bryan said. "You should know that scouts for the baseball summer camp are here."

Sam's eyes widened. "Really? No wonder those guys did this. I guess I'd better pitch well. I've only got an inning to show my stuff."

"Way to go, Sammy," Bryan said. "I'm making a film about this one day."

"Cool!" Sam said. "Cast Tom Cruise as me. Now let's go win a ball game!"

The kids, the umpire, and even Mr. Leblanc raced back to the field to loud cheers.

"Knock 'em dead, Sammy!" Mr. Hanraddy cried.

"Good to see you, Sam," Mr. Lester said, pumping his arm. "Get these three outs, and your ERA falls below two."

Bryan crouched behind the plate while Sam threw a few warm-up pitches.

Zing!

The first pitch rocketed into Bryan's glove.

"Lookin' very sharp," Bryan yelled.

"Way to go, Sammy," Peter said as he trotted out to take Marla's position in left field.

Sam smiled. He felt a surge of raw power. He was raring to go.

A runner was on second in Kevin's place, and the score was 9–4. Kevin and Larry were sitting on the bench, but even without them, the Hornet lineup was dangerous. Sam blew on his hand and turned toward the first batter, Larry's substitute.

He knew he should feel nervous, but he felt completely relaxed. Bryan called for a fastball on the outside corner of the plate. Sam wound up and threw.

"Striiike one!"

"Randy Johnson, step aside!" shouted Mr. Hanraddy.

As soon as Sam got the ball back he was ready to pitch again. He liked to work fast, without long pauses between pitches. Bryan called for a change-up over the inside corner. Sam nodded and let it rip.

The ball just nicked the plate. The batter overswung and hit a dribbler down the third-base line. Sam ducked as Nelson lunged after the ball and made an off-balance throw. The ball smacked into Corey's glove a second before the batter's foot touched first.

"Out!" cried the umpire.

"Nice," Sam called to Nelson.

Nelson gave the thumbs-up sign, and Sam turned to face the next batter, the boy with the fake tattoo.

"Hum it in here, baby," Bryan called. "You've got the stuff."

Sam wound up and zinged a ball in for strike one. Another pitch, another strike. And then, *whiff!*

"Striiike three!" the ump called, pumping his arm like a piston. "You are out of there!"

Bryan threw the ball around the horn. Sam felt his heart pounding. One more batter, and the Sonics could try for a comeback.

The Paul Bunyan look-alike stepped up to the plate. He hadn't had much luck today, but Sam knew he was one of the Hornets' toughest outs. Sam didn't want to groove a fastball over the plate. If he did, it would be shot out of the park like a cannonball.

Bryan got into his crouch and signaled

for an inside fastball. Sam nodded. It was his best pitch. A power hitter against a power pitcher.

Well, Sam thought, *if he can hit my best stuff out, good for him.*

He wound up and threw.

"Striiike one!"

"Way to hum it, Sam baby!" Mr. Hanraddy shouted.

"Two more like those!" Bryan yelled. "Let's go. Show him your stuff, Sam."

The Hornet tapped his cleats with his bat and stepped back into the box.

"Come on!" Coach Anderchuk yelled. "Get us some insurance. This boy isn't that good."

Sam smiled and let another pitch rocket home.

"Ball one!" the ump cried.

Bryan tossed it back. Sam rubbed the ball as he watched the batter work dirt into his hands. Sam's palms were sweaty, but the ball felt good. He was in total control.

Another windup—this time it was a pitch he rarely threw, a curve.

The batter took a mighty swing but was ahead of it and drove it foul down the third-base line.

"One and two!" the umpire shouted.

"Come on, Sam, get this last one," Corey called from first.

The crowd was on the edge of their seats. Sam wiped his brow. Bryan called for a fastball. Sam nodded. Heart thumping, he toed the rubber, wound up, and threw.

Swing!

Thud! The ball resounded from deep in the pocket of Bryan's glove.

"Striiike three!" the umpire called. "Yer out of there!"

Sam whooped for joy and dashed off the field.

SONIC REVENGE

"Now we need some runs," Sam said. "Who's up?"

"Top of the order," Mr. Lester said. "That's you, Jack. Come on, now, get us started."

The crowd was on its feet. Even though the Sonics needed five runs to tie, there was something electric in the air, like anything was possible.

"Watch out, Hornets!" Jack shouted as he reached for his bat.

"Nickel-and-dime 'em," Mr. Hanraddy

advised. "Don't try to get it all back at once."

"Here we go!"

"Do it!"

The Hornets were ready, but with two substitutes in the field for Larry and Kevin.

From the first pitch, the Sonics were like a new team. They were unstoppable. First Jack drove a hard shot up the middle for a single. Then Lara lined a double down the right-field line to bring Jack speeding home. Nelson, who'd had a rough day at the plate, came through big time: a solid single to left, scoring Lara.

Runner on first, two runs in, no outs. Sam watched and cheered from the dugout. It looked like he was going to get his chance to bat.

"Come on, Corey," he cried. "Do it!"

Corey smiled. The pitch came in, and Corey squared. With a deft punch of the bat, the ball rolled slowly up the third-base line.

"Safe!" the umpire called.

"Beautiful!" Mr. Lester called. "That was your ninth successful bunt of the season. Superb!"

Butterflies were beginning to churn in Sam's belly. He was batting in Marla's place, before Peter. He was up right after Bryan, who was next. He looked toward the scouts in the stands and gulped.

"Go for it!" Sam said, slapping Bryan on the back. "Smack one."

But the Hornet pitcher was getting riled. His first three pitches were definitely unsmackable. Three balls.

Bryan sighed. "Come on!" he yelled. "Gimme something I can get the wood onto!"

Bryan smoked the next pitch through the right side of the infield. Nelson chugged home, and Corey moved all the way to third.

"Excellent!" Mr. Lester called. "Three runs in."

Hornets 9, Sonics 7. Now it was Sam's turn.

"All right, Sammy," Mr. Hanraddy cautioned, "don't try to get it all back at once. Just make contact."

"Downtown, baby!" someone in the stands called. "A homer wins it!"

The crowd was on their feet, cheering.

Sam felt his heart jump. He knew he represented the winning run. What better ending?—the boy who was locked in a closet coming back to win it all with a single swing.

"Say," the Hornet catcher said as Sam dug into the batter's box. "You could be a real hero, you know?"

"Yeah," Sam said. "I know."

"Don't be too nervous. . . ."

"Who's nervous?" Sam replied.

But his voice shook, and the butterflies were doing cartwheels. He had to relax. His pounding heart was ringing in his ears, and a thin line of sweat trickled down his back.

The pitcher took the sign, and Sam got ready. The crowd hushed. The first pitch came in low and fast. Sam thought it was too low, but the ump thought differently.

"Striiike one!"

Sam stepped back out of the box and took a deep breath.

"That's all right, Sammy," Mr. Lester cried. "Wait for your highest-percentage pitch."

"Home run! Home run!" the crowd chanted.

Sam rubbed dirt on his hands and stepped back into the box. The pitcher took the sign and threw. This time the ball was definitely too low, and the ump agreed.

"Ball one!"

"Go for it, Sammy!" Corey cried from third. "Hit me in."

"You can do it, Sammy!" Bryan yelled.

"Make it happen!"

"Get a good piece of it!"

"Relax up there!"

"Wait for your pitch!"

"Keep your back elbow up!"

"Don't overswing!"

"Just a little hit. No big deal!"

But it was a big deal. Advice rattled through Sam's head like a speeding train. It was nearly impossible to relax, to concentrate.

Man, he thought, *think how much pressure major leaguers must feel.*

He willed himself to stay focused, to block out the noise, to forget about the broom closet, the inning he had just pitched, the excitement of going to baseball camp. . . . The only things he saw were the pitcher, the ball, and the bat— nothing else.

Come on, he thought. *Try to blow one by me.*

The Hornet pitcher wheeled back and threw a hard fastball. Again, the ball was coming in low. Sam knew the umpire had called the first low pitch a strike. He watched the ball come closer and closer. Then he saw his bat whip around and make perfect contact with the ball.

CRACK!

The liner took off like a rocket and crashed into the left-field fence. Corey scored easily. Bryan ran as hard as he could, but had to stop at third. Sam stood on second with a thunderous double.

"Down by one!" Mr. Lester cried.

Now it was Peter's turn. The boy who had been wrongly accused stepped to the plate. The fans cheered even louder.

"Do it!" Lara cried.

"A hit wins it for us," Corey yelled.

"Pe-ter! Pe-ter!" Mr. Hanraddy began to chant.

Peter dug into the dirt. He was angry. He rubbed his hands in the dirt and took a practice cut. He dug his cleats into the batter's box and, with a hard glint in his eye, stared down the Hornets' pitcher.

"Wait for your pitch," Mr. Lester advised.

"You're a hitter!" Sam cried from second. "Bang me home!"

"Don't strand me," Bryan yelled from third.

Peter blocked out all the noise. His heart was racing, but it wasn't fear. The Hornet pitcher wound up. The pitch came in: a fastball.

"Striiike one!" the ump called.

Peter stepped back out of the box.

"All right, Peter," Mr. Lester called. "Wait for yours."

"Hit ze ball!" Mr. Leblanc cried.

"Good wood!" Mr. Hanraddy called. "Good wood!"

Everyone was on their feet, including the scouts. This had turned into some game.

Peter stepped back into the batter's box. His shoulder still ached from the day's pitching, but he wasn't going to let that stop him now.

"Get ready to strike out," the Hornet catcher said.

The pitcher fired in another. Peter saw it clearly and, with a mighty swing, sent it flying over the third baseman's head.

A clean single!

Bryan scored, Sam rounded third.

"Go!" Mr. Lester called.

The crowd gasped. The Hornet left fielder whipped the ball home.

"Slide!" Lara yelled.

"Hit the dirt!" Jack cried.

The Hornet catcher was blocking the plate, waiting for the throw. He caught it and spun around. Sam slid, hooking the plate with his toe. A plume of dust and dirt shot into the air. The ump hesitated, narrowed his eyes, then yelled out his verdict.

"SAFE!"

The next thing both Sam and Peter knew, they were being mobbed.

"Way to go!" Lara yelled to Peter, slapping his back. "Game-winning ribbie!"

"*Excellent!*" Mr. Leblanc shouted, giving

his nephew a hug. "Your mother will be so proud."

"Nice slide," Mr. Lester told Sam. "My statistics tell me that . . ."

The next five minutes were total chaos. Cheers shook the small stands. Even Hornet fans applauded. The five friends exchanged high fives. Fans hugged one another. The umpire took off his mask and grinned.

Sam felt a tap on his shoulder.

The two scouts! Sam's heart began to thump. The woman extended her hand.

"Nice job," she said. "Clutch playing."

"Thanks."

The other scout nodded. "Nice fastball and excellent change-up." He paused, then smiled. "If it's all right, we'd like to see what you can do when you haven't just been kidnapped."

"That's right," the other scout said. "Got any summer plans?"

Moments later, Sam was back with his team.

118

"You made it!" Jack cried.

"You'll show Kirby Puckett a thing or two at camp," Bryan said.

"Strike him out every time," Corey joked.

"What an amazing game!" Bryan said.

"Perfect!" Lara said.

"Unbelievable!" Jack added.

"The best game ever!" Sam declared.

Suddenly Bryan began to laugh. "Wow, Sam. That's pretty incredible. I mean, you spent most of this game in a supply room."

"But still, it's true." Sam shook himself. "What a game," he said. He looked around and gave himself a moment to take in the cheering fans, the umpire, the Hornets, the scouts, the glory of it all. "What an *incredible* game!"